the BAD GUYS

EPISODE

1

• FOR MY BOYS •

SCHOLASTIC CHILDREN'S BOOKS
AN IMPRINT OF SCHOLASTIC LTD
EUSTON HOUSE, 24 EVERSHOLT STREET, LONDON, NW1 1DB, UK
REGISTERED OFFICE: WESTFIELD ROAD, SOUTHAM, WARWICKSHIRE, CV47 0RA
SCHOLASTIC AND ASSOCIATED LOGOS ARE TRADEMARKS AND/OR REGISTERED TRADEMARKS
OF SCHOLASTIC INC.

FIRST PUBLISHED IN AUSTRALIA BY SCHOLASTIC AUSTRALIA, 2015
FIRST PUBLISHED IN THE UK BY SCHOLASTIC LTD, 2016

ISBN 978 1407 17056 5

A CIP CATALOGUE RECORD FOR THIS BOOK IS AVAILABLE FROM THE BRITISH LIBRARY.

PRINTED BY CPI GROUP (UK) LTD, CROYDON, CR0 4YY
PAPERS USED BY SCHOLASTIC CHILDREN'S BOOKS ARE MADE FROM WOOD GROWN IN
SUSTAINABLE FORESTS.

1 3 5 7 9 10 8 6 4 2

WWW.SCHOLASTIC.CO.UK

· AARON BLABEY ·

the BAD GUYS

EPISODE 1

SCHOLASTIC

GOOD DEEDS.

WHETHER YOU LIKE
IT OR NOT.

· CHAPTER 1 ·
MR WOLF

Pssst!
Hey, you!

Yeah, you.

Get over here.

I said, **GET OVER HERE**.

What's the problem?

Oh, I see.

Yeah, I get it . . .

You're thinking, 'Ooooooh, it's a big, bad, scary wolf! I don't want to talk to him!

He's a **MONSTER**.'

Grandma?

Well, let me tell you something, buddy –
just because I've got

BIG POINTY TEETH and RAZOR SHARP CLAWS

. . . and I *occasionally* like to dress up
like an **OLD LADY**, that doesn't mean . . .

. . . I'm a

BAD GUY.

METROPOLITAN POLICE DEPARTMENT

SUSPECT RAP SHEET

Name: Mr Wolf

Case Number: 102 451A

Alias: Big Bad, Mr Choppers, Grandma

Address: The Woods

Known Associates: None

Criminal Activity:

* Blowing down houses (the three pigs involved were too scared to press charges)

* Impersonating sheep

* Breaking into the homes of old women

* Impersonating old women

* Attempting to eat old women

* Attempting to eat relatives of old women

* Theft of nighties and slippers

Status: Dangerous. DO NOT APPROACH

It's all **LIES**, I tell you.

But you don't believe me, do you?

Because I'm The Bad Guy, right?

I'm a great guy. A *nice* guy, even.

But I'm not just talking about **ME** . . .

I've got some buddies who have the same problem, so I've asked them to join us.

Any minute now, they'll be walking right through that door.

They're great guys. But just like me, they are **MISUNDERSTOOD**.

So don't go anywhere, OK?

· CHAPTER 2 ·
THE GANG

OK. Are you ready
to learn the truth?

You'd better be, baby.

Let's see who's here,
shall we?

Heeey! Look who it is!
It's my good pal,

MR SNAKE.

You're going to *love* him.
He's a real . . .

. . . sweetheart.

METROPOLITAN
POLICE DEPARTMENT
SUSPECT RAP SHEET

Name: Mr Snake

Case Number: 354 22C

Alias: The Chicken Swallower

Address: Unknown

Known Associates: None

Criminal Activity: * Broke into Mr Ho's Pet Store

* Ate all the mice at Mr Ho's Pet Store

* Ate all the canaries at Mr Ho's Pet Store

* Ate all the guinea pigs at Mr Ho's Pet Store

* Tried to eat Mr Ho at Mr Ho's Pet Store

* Tried to eat the doctor who tried to save Mr Ho

* Tried to eat the policemen who tried to save the doctor who tried to save Mr Ho

* Ate the police dog who tried to save the policemen who tried to save the doctor who tried to save Mr Ho

Status: Very Dangerous. DO NOT APPROACH

Look at this face!
Is this the face of a monster?

I don't think so.

This is **ONE SWEET GUY**.

Will this take long, man?
I've got mice to eat.

What a joker this guy is!

'I've got mice to eat!'
That's a good one.

What a wise guy.

HA HA HA.

HA.

HA.

Take it easy.
Have a cupcake.

A cupcake?
You got
any mice?

Enough with the mice,
or I'll

EAT
YOU!

I mean . . .

Well, well. If it isn't

MR PIRANHA.

Now, if anyone has
a bad reputation,
it's this guy . . .

Hola.

METROPOLITAN POLICE DEPARTMENT

SUSPECT RAP SHEET

Name: Mr Piranha

Case Number: 775 906T

Alias: The Bum Muncher

Address: The Amazon River

Known Associates: The Piranha Brothers Gang 900,543 members, all related to Mr Piranha

Criminal Activity:

* Eating tourists

Status: EXTREMELY Dangerous. DO NOT APPROACH

I've come all the way from Bolivia, hermanos.

And I'm hungry! So where's the

MEAT?

HAHA!
These guys are killing me!
Always with the jokes!

No meat.

Just cake.

KNOCK! KNOCK!

KNOCK!

AHA! Now I know **THIS** guy likes cake . . .

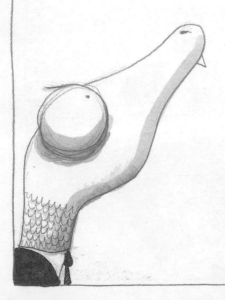

32

Hey there, **MR SHARK**.
How's it going?

I'm

HUNGRY

You got any

seals?

Okey dokey. Nothing to see here . . .

METROPOLITAN POLICE DEPARTMENT

SUSPECT RAP SHEET

Name: Mr Shark

Case Number: 666 885E

Alias: Jaws

Address: Popular Tourist Destinations

* Will literally eat ANYTHING or ANYBODY.

Status: RIDICULOUSLY DANGEROUS. RUN! SWIM! DON'T EVEN READ THIS! GET OUT OF HERE!!

See?! This is what I'm talking about! How will anyone take us seriously as

GOOD GUYS

if all you want to do is

EAT EVERYONE?

Good guys?
What's
he talking
about?

Beats me . . .

What am I **TALKING** about?

Well, sit down and I'll explain.

And that means *you*, too.

· CHAPTER 3 ·
the GOOD GUYS CLUB

AAAAIIIIEEEEEE!!!!!!!

Typical . . .

Hey, shouldn't you two be in water?

I'll be wherever I want.

Got it?

Me too, chico.

See? This is why
I don't work with fish.

Because **THIS** is the very first meeting of . . .

THE
GOOD
GUYS
CLUB!

That's right!

The
GOOD
GUYS
CLUB!

47

I beg your pardon?

You heard me.

Aren't you tired of being the
VILLAIN?

Aren't you tired of the
SCREAMS?

Aren't you tired of the
FEAR?

Not particularly.

Not in the slightest.

OF COURSE YOU ARE!

And I have the solution!

POP QUIZ! Let's say we find a cat stuck up a tree.

What do we do?

This guy's loco.

No, I'm not!

I'm a GENIUS!

And I'm going to make us all

HEROES!

He's completely lost his mind.

I came all the
way from Bolivia
for THIS?

You'll be glad you did, Mr Piranha.

And so will you, Mr Shark.

This is going to be **AWESOME.**

Now, everybody climb aboard!

And let's go do some

GOOD!

· CHAPTER 4 ·
CRUISING FOR TROUBLE

This car is a fuel-injected,
200-HORSE-POWER,
rock'n'rollin' chariot of
flaming **COOLNESS**, my friend.
If we're going to be good guys,
don't you think we should
LOOK GOOD too?

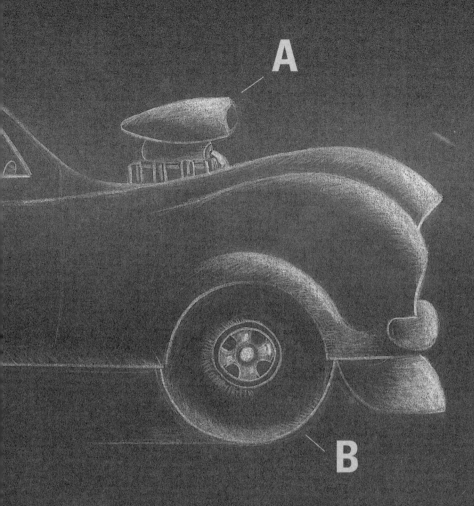

A - 'Fully Sick' V8 Engine that runs on undiluted panther wee.

B - Fat Wheels for just looking insanely cool.

C - Custom Ejector Seats for personal safety and also practical jokes.

D - Oversized Muffler for being very, very loud at all times.

And it's roomy, too!

Hey, it's a sweet ride, chico. But I get carsick, man. So what ARE we doing out here?

We need to be able to **SMELL** trouble!

In fact . . . wait a second . . . I think I can smell trouble right now . . .

Wow, it's really strong, actually . . .

Hang on. That's not . . .

AW, WHO FARTED?!

Actually, that feels quite nice.

Seriously though, man . . . what are we looking for?

SCREEEECH!

THAT is what we're looking for, Mr Snake!

· CHAPTER 5 ·
HERE, KITTY

So, what are we going to do?

Rescue the cat.

And what are we **NOT** going to do?

Eat the cat.

THAT'S RIGHT! I don't know about you, but I feel PUMPED!

OK, now let's do this thing . . .

What was *that*? Are you trying to give him a heart attack?

WHAT? I was, like, being totally cool . . .

Let me handle this.

HEY, YOU!

Get down here,

or I'll **SHIMMY**

up that tree and

BITE you

on your

FURRY

LITTLE

BUTT!

What's the matter with you?!

Well, someone had better do something. That screaming is getting on my nerves . . .

MUNCH!

HEY!

Where's the piranha?

I don't know
what you're
talking about.

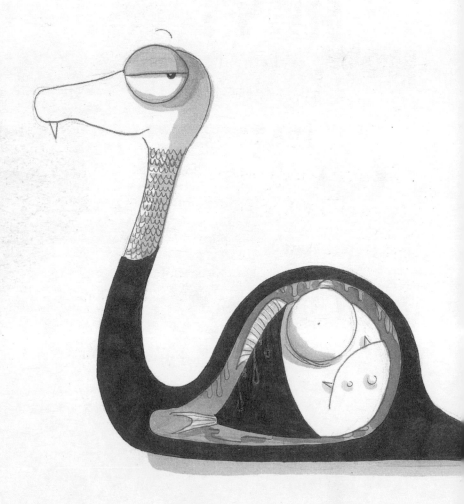

NOW,

please don't be alarmed.

It's true,

snakes can be tricky and they do tend to

swallow things that take their fancy.

BUT – luckily, they swallow them *whole*

and I happen to know a gentle,

harmless technique that'll fix this right up.

Excuse me for one moment . . .

I SAID . . .

WHERE'S

THE PIRANHA?!

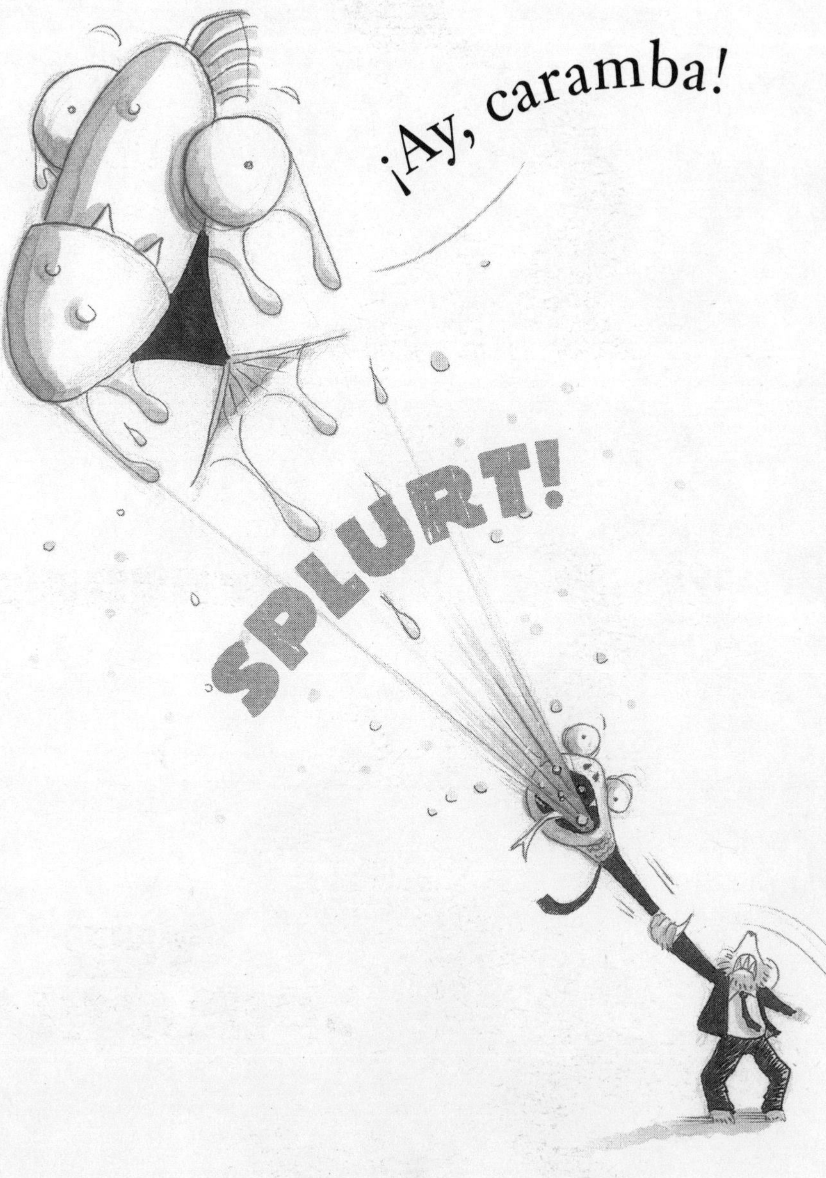
¡Ay, caramba!
SPLURT!

Hey, chico.
What's cookin'?

MEEEEEE

. . .EOW!

THAT'S IT!

I've got you,
I've got you . . .

· CHAPTER 6 ·
THE PLAN

Nice work.
High fives,
all 'round!

You're the only
one with hands.

Fair enough.

GROUP HUG?

I don't hug. I bite.
So **BACK OFF**,
Mr Snuggles.

Okey dokey . . .

Ready for what?

Well, I don't know about you, but I'd say we're **READY**.

Our first mission.

It's time for

OPERATION DOG POUND!

THE

534

10

200 DOGS

DOG POUND

20 GUARDS ←

ONE WAY IN.
ONE WAY OUT.

IRON BARS!
RAZOR WIRE!
BAD FOOD!

There are **200** puppies locked up in the

**MAXIMUM SECURITY
CITY DOG POUND.**

Their hopes and dreams are trapped
behind walls of stone and bars of steel.

But guess what?

We're going to

SET THEM FREE!

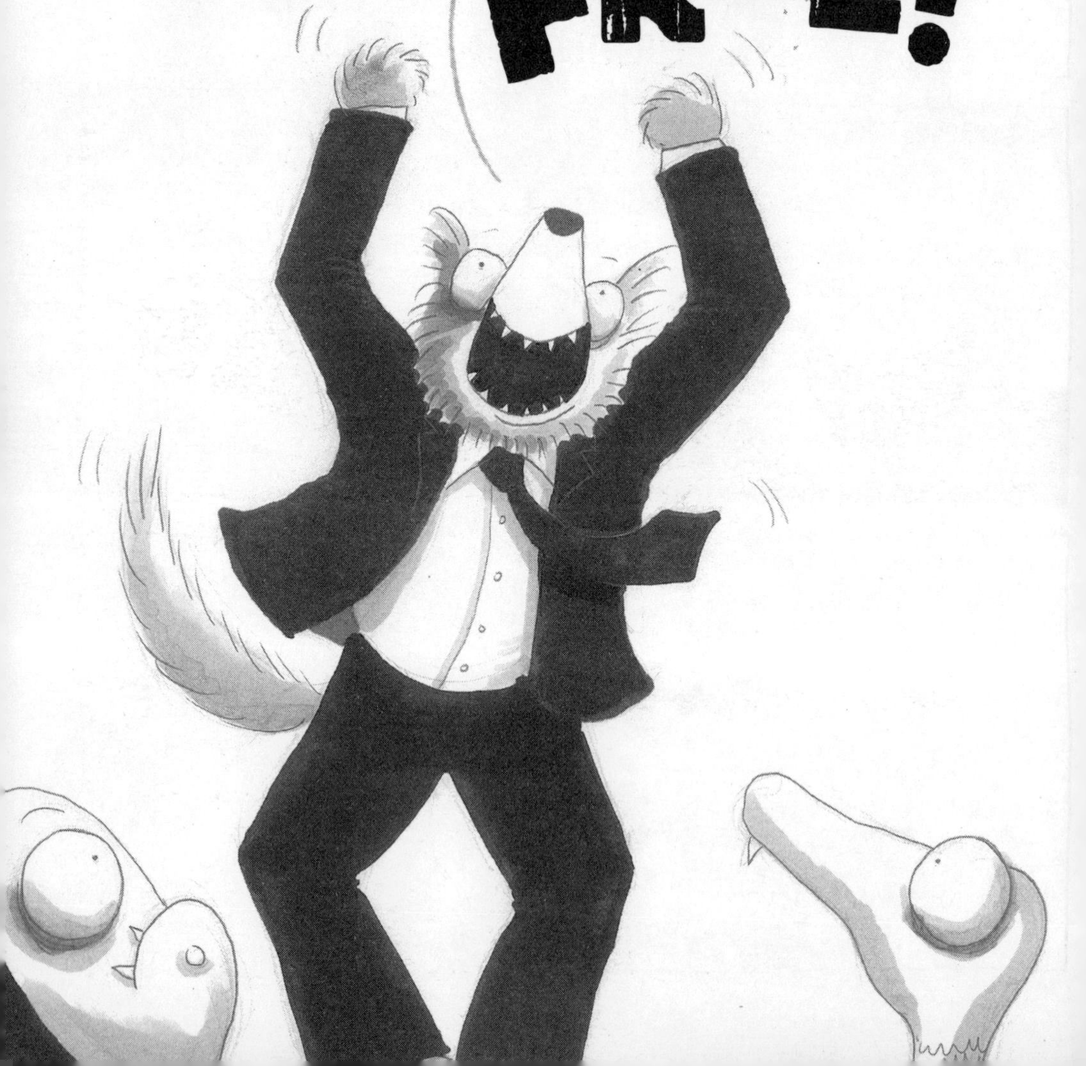

We couldn't get a kitten out of a tree. How are we supposed to bust out 200 dogs?

It's easy! One of us just has to get in there and open the cages!

And how do we do that?

With
THIS!

Are you going to dress up like an old lady AGAIN? It doesn't work, man. You ALWAYS get caught!

Who said anything about *me*?

· CHAPTER 7 ·
THE POUND

Hullo?
Oh, certainly Miss.
I'll buzz you in.

BUZZZ!

Now, what can I do
for . . . uh . . . you?

I'm just a pretty young lady who has lost her dog.
Please, oh please, can you help me, sir?

Well, OF COURSE!

Anything for such a lovely young lass.

Cool.

He's in!
I **KNEW** this
would work.

Now, you know what to do.
Once those cages are open,
we won't have long,
so don't mess it up.

Climb aboard, fellas!

What's that
thing for?

Never you mind. Just hold on tight.
And remember – once Mr Shark
gives me the signal, I'll get you
inside and all you have to do is tell
the dogs which way to run.

GOT IT?

Yeah. But
how do we
get inside?

But don't worry!

I have **EXCELLENT** aim

and I'm **85%** sure

that I'll get you in on my first throw –

THAT'S

how confident I am!

You know, I
wouldn't normally
open all these
cages at once,
but since you
asked so nicely . . .

Well, here's the last cage.
Is THIS your dog?

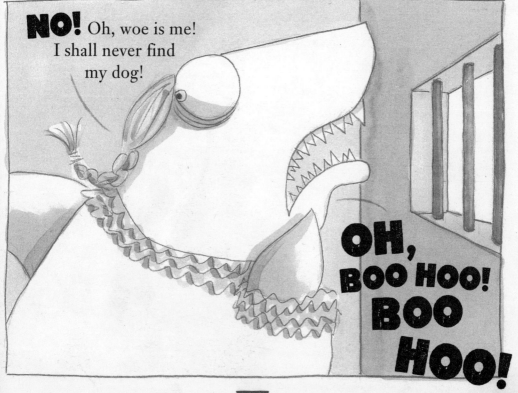

NO! Oh, woe is me!
I shall never find
my dog!

OH,
BOO HOO!
BOO
HOO!

That's the signal!

Hey, man, can we talk
about this for a second?

There's no time to talk! Hold on tight, little buddies.

It's time . . .

to go

BE A HERO!

SWOOSH!

OK.
Best out of three.

YEAH.
I'm getting the
hang of it now . . .

SPLAT!

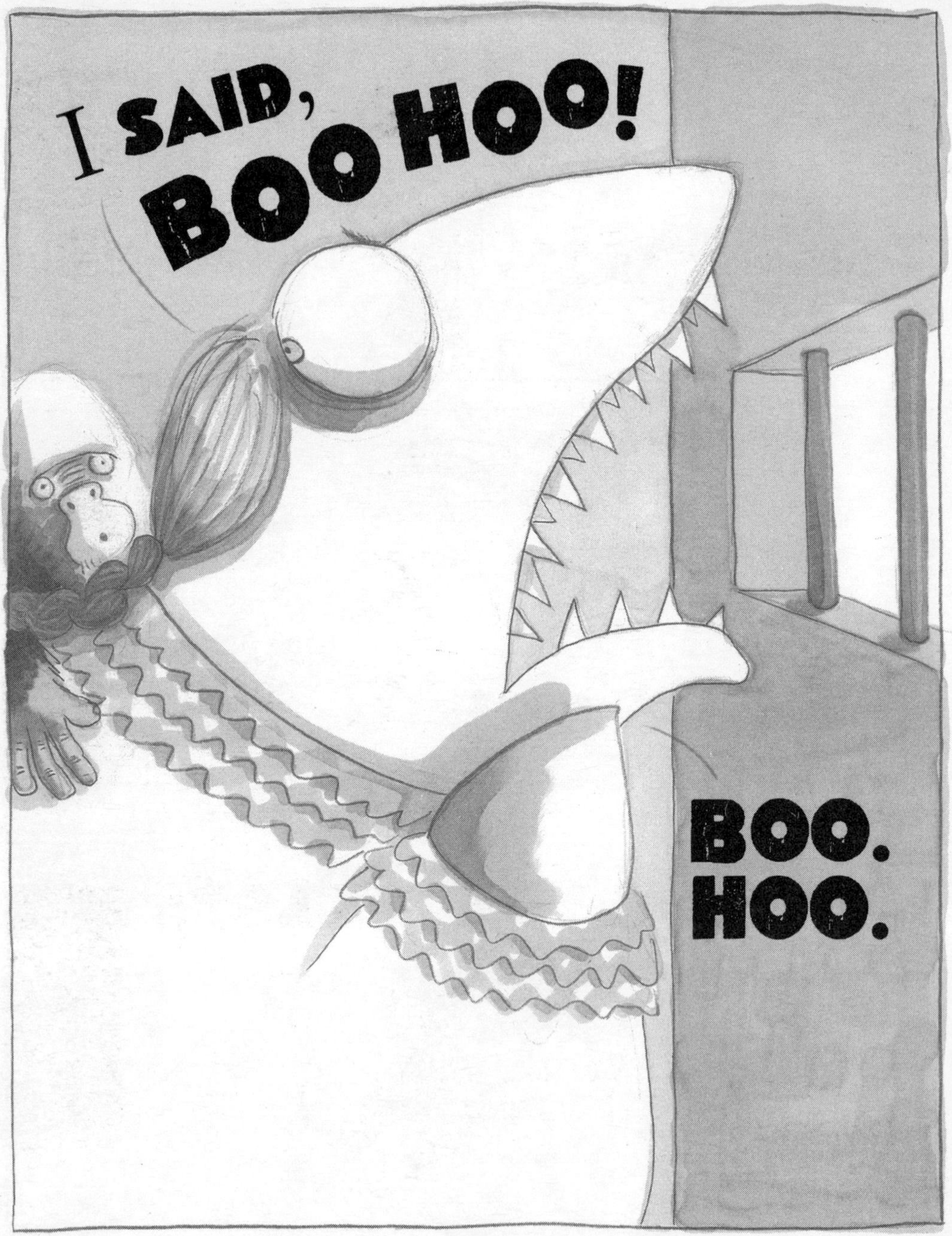
I SAID, BOO HOO!
BOO. HOO.

I'm sorry, young lady, but I'd better lock these cages back up now.

THIS. IS. GOING. TO. WORK.

If we survive this, I'm going to *eat* that wolf.

Not if I do first.

OK, fellas!
Back in your cages.

We're **NOT** going to make it.

We're **NOT** going to make it.

We're **NOT** going to make it.

We're **NOT** going to make it.

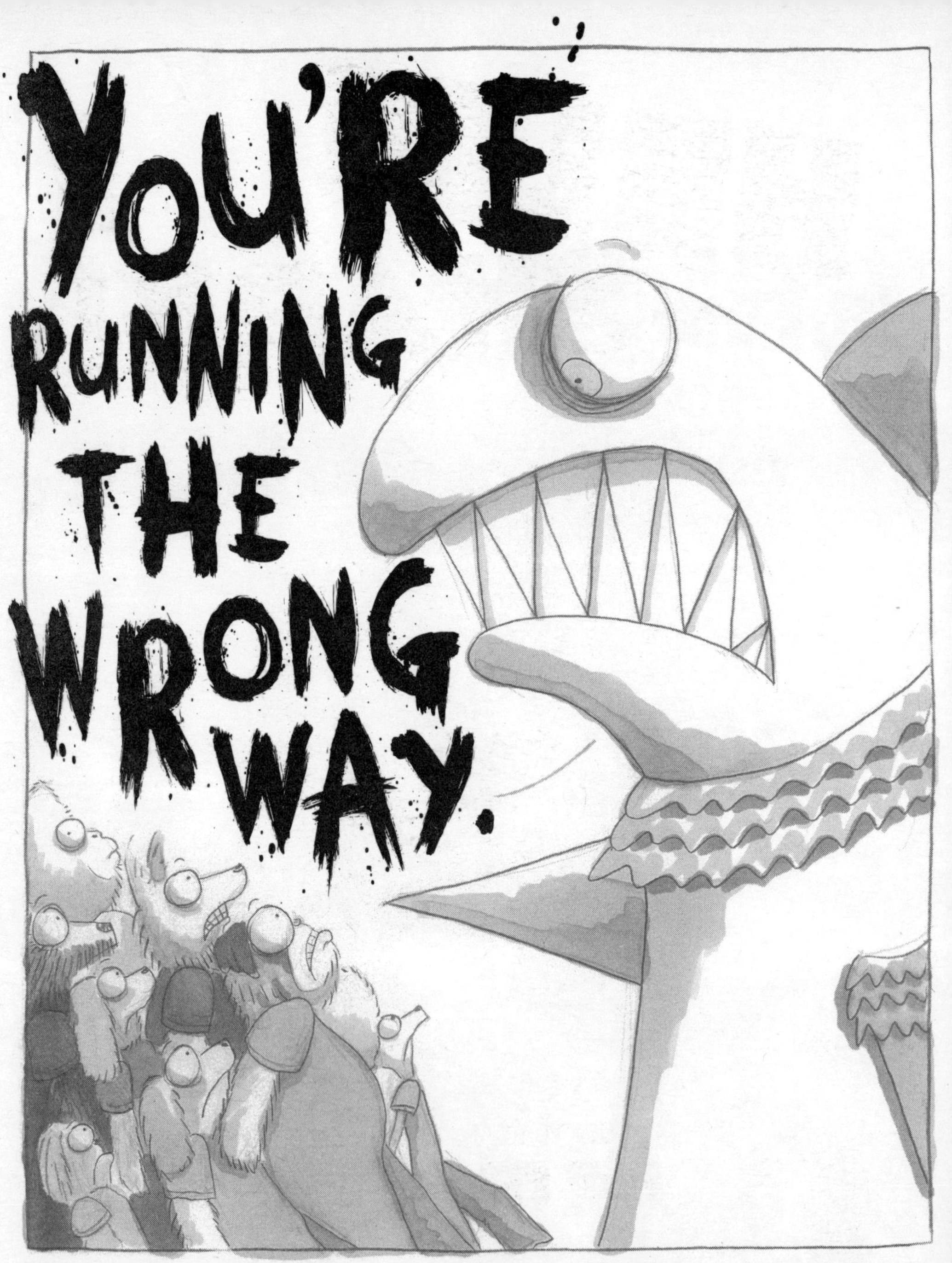
YOU'RE RUNNING THE WRONG WAY.

HELP! SHARK!

That
did it!

OK,
MR WOLF . . .
HIT IT!

I hear you,
little buddy.

Let's give those puppies their . . .

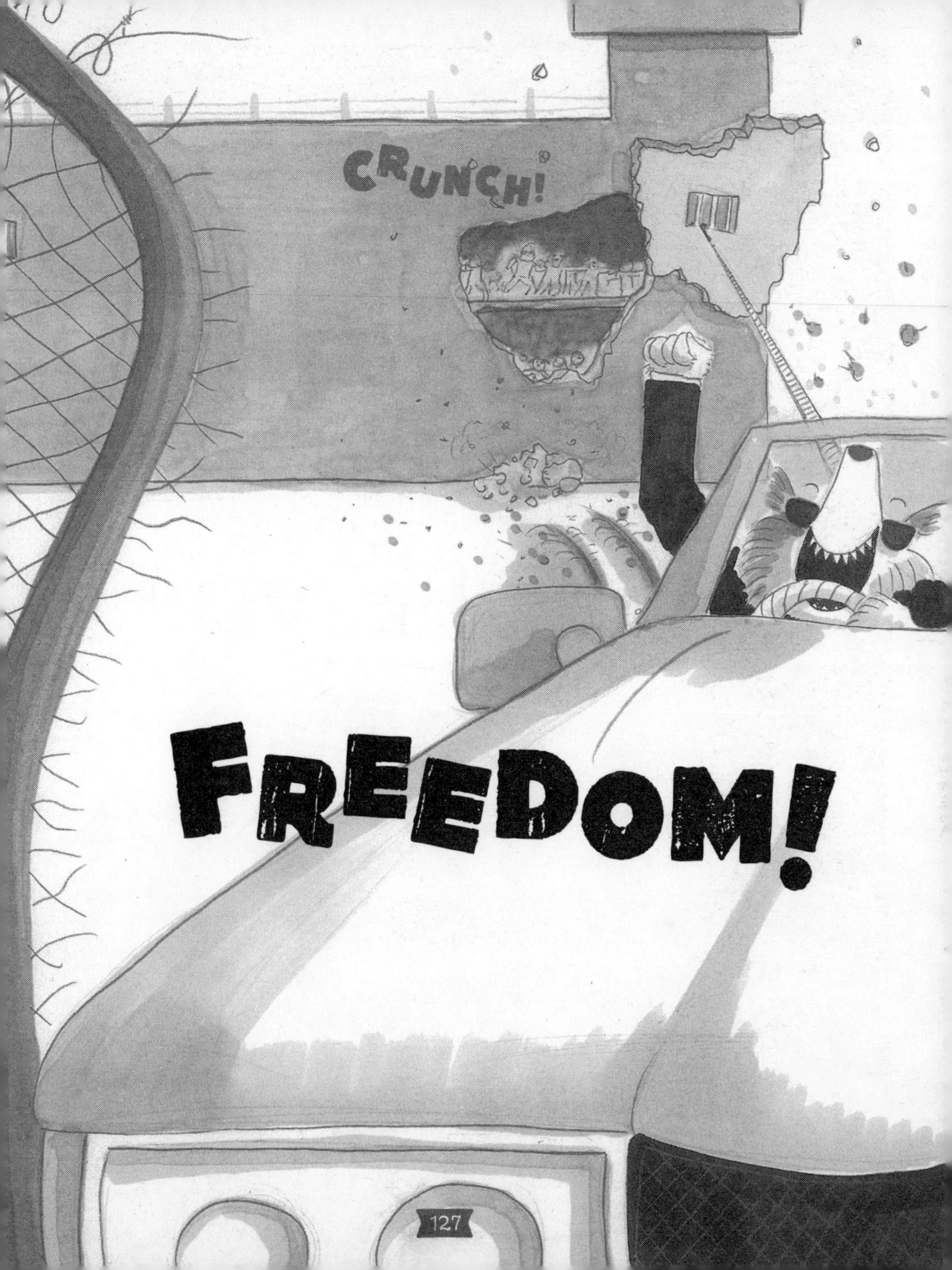
CRUNCH!
FREEDOM!

And a SHARK!
And a SNAKE!
And possibly some kind of VAMPIRE SARDINE!
224

CHAPTER 8

SO, HOW ABOUT IT?

Well, they certainly didn't seem very grateful, did they?

They called me a SARDINE!

I thought you WERE a sardine.

I'm not a SARDINE! I'M A PIRANHA, man! **PIRANHA!**

Whatever.

You're missing the point, guys. **WE DID IT!** We gave 200 dogs a whole new life. Doesn't that just make you feel **AWESOME?!**

You really do hug WAY more than I'm comfortable with, man.

Aw, **C'MON!**

You loved it! I KNOW you did!

Tell me the truth – didn't it feel great

to be the **GOOD GUY** for once?

Tell me how it felt, fellas . . .

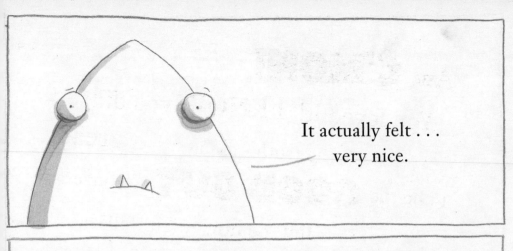

It actually felt . . .
very nice.

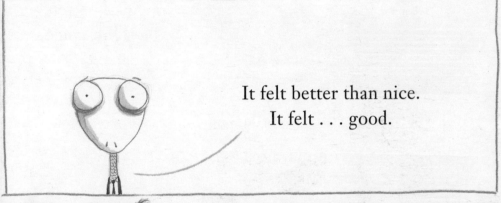

It felt better than nice.
It felt . . . good.

It felt **WONDERFUL**, man.
But they still called me a SARDINE!!!

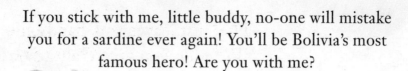

If you stick with me, little buddy, no-one will mistake you for a sardine ever again! You'll be Bolivia's most famous hero! Are you with me?

Sure. But you'd better be right, chico.

And what about you, big fella?

I . . . I really liked being good. I'm in.

That just leaves you, handsome.
What do you say? Want to be
in my gang?

Only if I have your word that
there'll be no more hugging.

I'll try, baby! But I'm not
making any promises!

Today is the first day of our **new** lives.

We are **not** Bad Guys anymore.

WE'RE
GOOD GUYS!

And we are going to make the
world a **better** place.

For the first time in my life . . .
the future smells sweet!

Wait a second –

That doesn't
smell sweet . . .

Piranha, did you
fart *again*?

I get gassy when I'm
upset. Just deal with
it, chico.

TO BE CONTINUED . . .